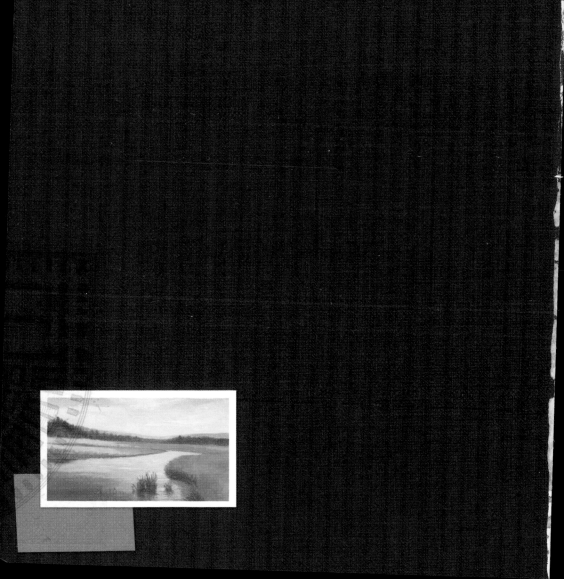

To My Dad

With love,

_____

Published by Hallmark Books,
a division of Hallmark Cards, Inc.,
Kansas City, MO 64141
Visit us on the Web at www.Hallmark.com.

Editor: Theresa Trinder
Art Director: Kevin Swanson
Designer: Sarah Smitka - The Pink Pear Design Co.
Production Artist: Dan Horton

ISBN 978-1-59530-306-6

BOK2112

Printed and bound in China

To My Dad

THANKS

for Everything

Fig. 5

A ——————————— B
    C
    △

You're the *type of dad*
who's not a type at all.

You're not just a sports fan
or a disciplinarian or a goofball;
you're so many things on any given day.

And I realize now
that your complexity has given me
permission to be the same—
to be as many different versions
of me as I need to be.

You *supported* me.
You *challenged* me.

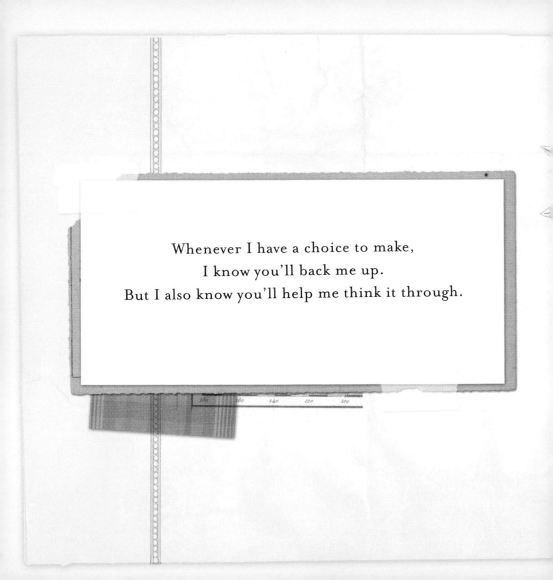

Whenever I have a choice to make,
I know you'll back me up.
But I also know you'll help me think it through.

You're not afraid to ask the tough questions.
To make me dig deeper. To make me think . . .

And whether I stand fast
or change my mind, I'm always
more certain of myself in the end.

You're a tough crowd, Dad.
If I can convince you,
I can convince anybody!

You *pushed* me.
You *praised* me.

You've always wanted the best for your family,
and that meant being the best you can be.
I learned this from you, Dad.

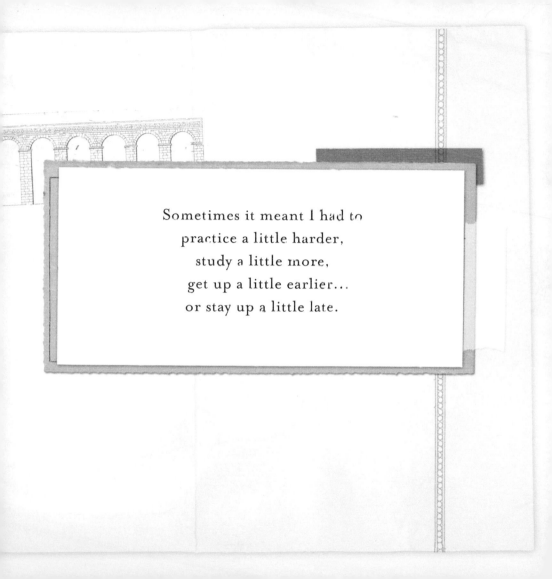

Sometimes it meant I had to
practice a little harder,
study a little more,
get up a little earlier...
or stay up a little late.

Sometimes it meant
you didn't let me quit.

But even when I felt defeated, you cheered me on. You always made me feel like my best was good enough.

And to this day, it is the reason I strive to make my best even better.

You made me *cautious*, and you made me *courageous*.

The world outside isn't always polite
or well-meaning; you knew that.

You gave me rules for a reason,
and now I understand
they weren't to keep me bored.
They were to keep me safe.

When the time came for me
to face some things on my own,
I wasn't afraid. You taught me to trust
my gut, honor my own opinion, and
to stand up for myself. Once in a while,
that meant standing up to you.

— 15°

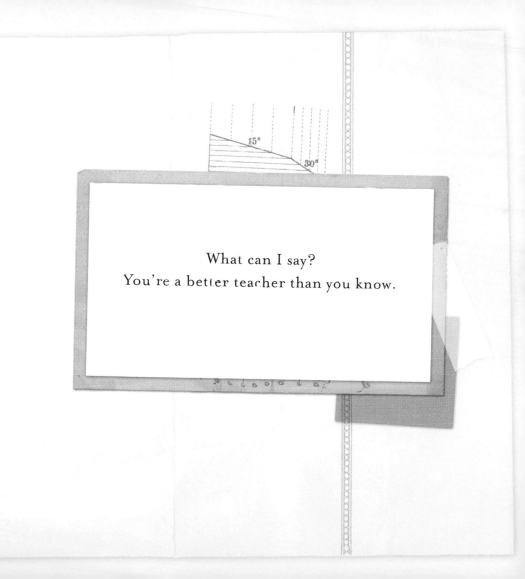

What can I say?
You're a better teacher than you know.

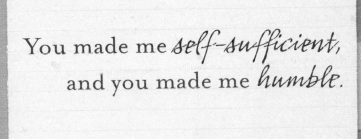

You made me *self-sufficient,*
and you made me *humble.*

From the first time I insisted
"I can do it"
you let me try things on my own.

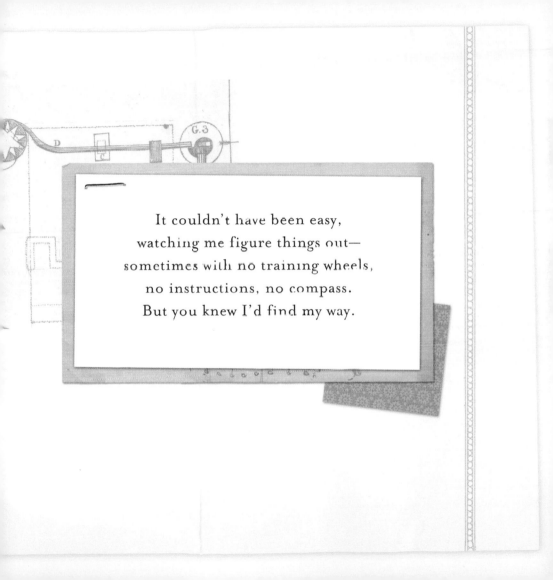

It couldn't have been easy,
watching me figure things out—
sometimes with no training wheels,
no instructions, no compass.
But you knew I'd find my way.

You trusted me,
and that helped me trust myself.

There were times when I couldn't do it alone,
and you taught me that sometimes
the best thing I can do for myself
is to ask someone for help.

You showed me
how to *earn my keep.*

You made sure I understood
that life doesn't owe me anything,
and whatever I want I have to work for.

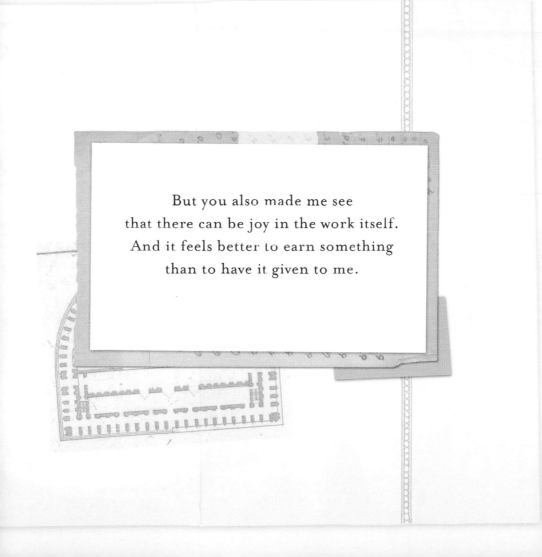

But you also made me see
that there can be joy in the work itself.
And it feels better to earn something
than to have it given to me.

I know how to give my all
to the task at hand.

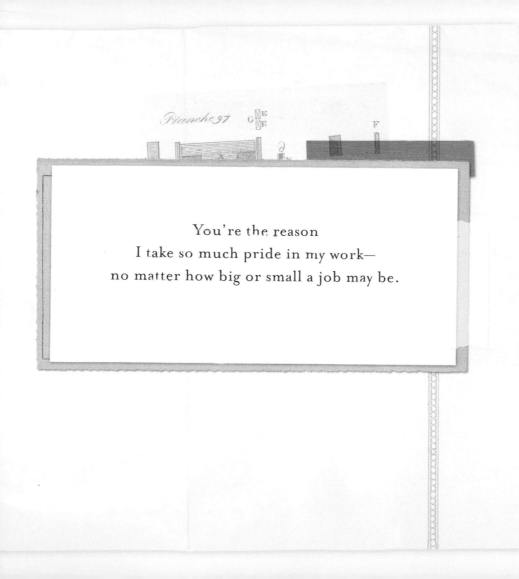

You're the reason
I take so much pride in my work—
no matter how big or small a job may be.

You showed me how
to *laugh it off.*

14

13

Take life seriously.
But don't take *yourself* too seriously.
That's a message you live loud and clear.

I learned a lot about balance from watching you. You showed me that work and home are both important, and while it can't always be exactly 50/50, I don't have to sacrifice one for the other.

When there was work to do, you gave every challenge your best—you were accountable. Sometimes you were stressed, but you tried not to bring it home with you. I guess that's what it means to "leave it on the field."

When you came home, we cracked jokes and played games. We relaxed a little, laughed a lot, and everybody felt better—no matter what happened during the day. That's why I know how important it is to have fun.

You taught me
about *family*.

Sometimes we fight with each other;
sometimes we fight *for* each other.
And we're about as quick to publicly brag
as we are to privately criticize.

Fig. 36

We laugh and cry, play and work,
and make a million memories in between.
That's what families do.

Family amplifies the good stuff
and helps drown out the bad.
We share it all—sometimes *too* much.

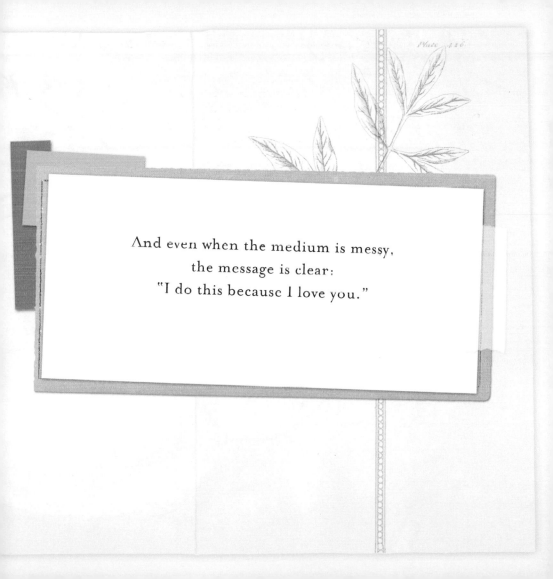

And even when the medium is messy,
the message is clear:
"I do this because I love you."

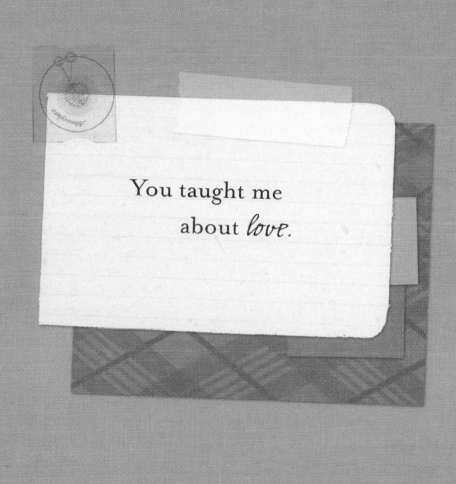

You taught me
about *love*.

If all we needed was love,
then life would be a lot easier.

But love won't get very far without
respect, understanding, humility,
and a good sense of humor.

For us, love is honest opinions and
the occasional "I told you so." It's doing without
so someone else can have and giving without
expecting anything in return.

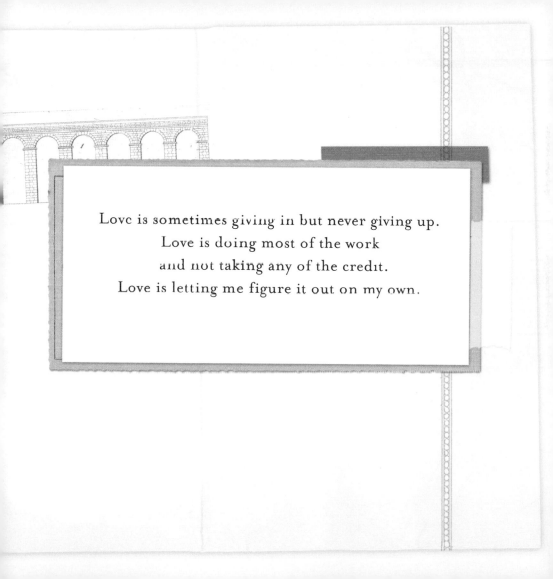

Love is sometimes giving in but never giving up.
Love is doing most of the work
and not taking any of the credit.
Love is letting me figure it out on my own.

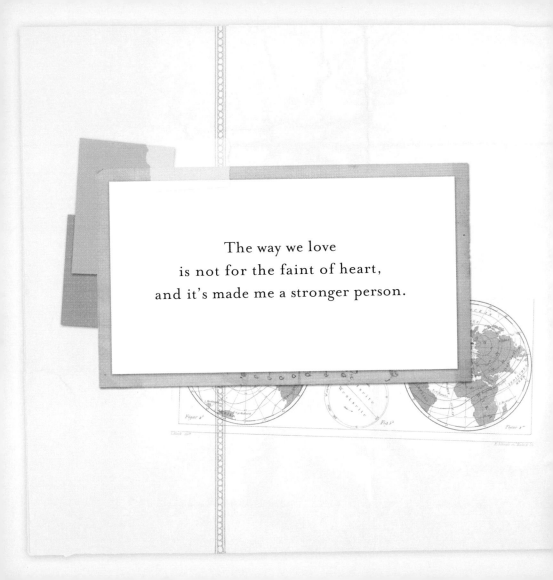

The way we love
is not for the faint of heart,
and it's made me a stronger person.

I know how to show love for others,
and I know how to love myself.
I have you to thank for that.

So maybe you didn't give me
everything I ever wanted,
but you gave me more than you know.

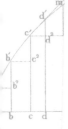

I don't know who I'd be without you, Dad,
but I probably wouldn't be
as funny or focused, as humble or
hardworking, as careful or confident.

15°

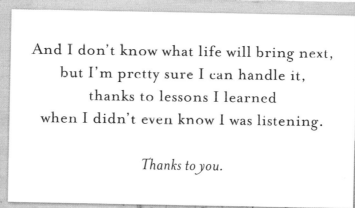

And I don't know what life will bring next,
but I'm pretty sure I can handle it,
thanks to lessons I learned
when I didn't even know I was listening.

Thanks to you.

If you have enjoyed this book
or it has touched your life
in some way, we would love
to hear from you.

Please send your comments to:
Hallmark Book Feedback
P.O. Box 419034
Mail Drop 215
Kansas City, MO 64141

Or e-mail us at:
booknotes@hallmark.com